CHANGING ROOMS

BY
MELANIE
JOYCE

ILLUSTRATED BY
ANDREW
WILDMAN

Learning Resource Service	
430580	
ASL F(7-11) FUL	

FULL FLIGHT

Titles in the Full Flight Heroes and Heroines series:

Badger Publishing Limited
Oldmedow Road,
Hardwick Industrial Estate,
King's Lynn PE30 4JJ
Telephone: 01438 791037
www.badgerlearning.co.uk

2 4 6 8 10 9 7 5 3 1

Changing Rooms ISBN 978 1 84926 478 5

Badger Publishing would like to thank Jonny Zucker for his help
in putting this series together.

Publisher: David Jamieson
Senior Editor: Danny Pearson
Design: Fiona Grant
Illustration: Andrew Wildman

CONTENTS

New words:

captain	costume
semi-final	locker
troupe	designed
listening	delivery
sewing	judge

Main characters:

Lisa  Tandy  Monica

CHAPTER 1
Beginnings

The Glitz final was weeks away.

Lisa couldn't believe it. Her dance troupe had made it through.

She was proud to be Captain. Dancing was her life.

Lisa looked at her old dance dress. She smiled. The new costumes would soon arrive.

Lisa couldn't wait. "We've got to win that final," she said.

"Who are you talking to?" said a voice.

It was Tandy.

It had been a hard practice.

"I just know we can win," said Lisa. "I can almost smell it. Everything has to be perfect," she said. "The moves, the costumes, everything."

"When will the costumes come?" said Tandy.

"Tomorrow, I hope," replied Lisa. "There are new dresses for you, me, Gina and Franky. Craig and Matt have got fantastic trousers and T-shirts. Watch out Monica Bleaks. Her Razor Edge team doesn't stand a chance. We're going to blow their socks off."

The two friends laughed.

Outside the door a shadow moved.

Beth was listening. She heard everything.

"If I tell Monica," she thought. "She'll let me dance in Razor Edge."

Beth crept carefully away. She hurried along the corridor.

Then she dashed through a door on the left.

Monica was in changing room two.
Beth ran in, breathless.

"What do you want?" said Monica.
She looked the girl up and down.

"The Candy Canes are going to win the
final," said Beth.

Monica's eyes flashed with anger.
Beth told her everything. Then Monica
grinned coldly.

"I like a challenge," she said.

CHAPTER 2
Order Form

Lisa waited for Tandy outside. It was getting dark.

She double-checked the costume order form. "Six super star troupe outfits. Hand beaded. Plus headpieces for the girls."

Everything looked perfect. Lisa put the order form in her bag.

The bag was heavy with school books. Suddenly, Lisa remembered. "I've left my essay in the locker," she thought.

Lisa put the bag on the floor. She ran inside to get her essay. Nearby, there were footsteps on the gravel. A gloved hand reached into the bag. It pulled out the order form. A voice read the words.

"Spotlight Costume Makers. Six super star troupe outfits. Hand beaded. Plus headpieces."

There was a strange laugh.

A mobile phone beeped.

Fingers pressed the key pad.
02891 684996.

On the other end, someone answered.
"Hello, Spotlight Costume Makers. Can I help you?"

The caller spoke.

"This is Lisa Edson. I need to make last minute changes to order number 30091."

The caller spoke quietly into the phone. Voices came from inside the dance school.

Suddenly, Lisa and Tandy came outside. Lisa reached down for her bag. The order form was lying beside it. "That's odd," said Lisa. "I'm sure I put it in my bag."

"It's been a long day," said Tandy. "Come on. Let's go home."

CHAPTER 3
Clown Tears

It was the last practice before the final. The Candy Canes went through their routine.

"Come on," said Lisa "Just one more time."

Monica sat at the edge of the hall.

She stared at the dancers. Beth sat next to her. "Can I be in Razor Edge?" she begged.

"Be quiet," snapped Monica.

Suddenly, the dance studio door opened. A man came in. He brought in two big boxes. "Delivery for Miss Lisa Edson."

"Can we open it?" said Lisa's troupe.

Lisa's heart beat fast. "Let's take it to the changing room!" she said.

The costumes had arrived.

The changing room was silent.

Lisa opened the box. Everyone waited. Then they saw her face. It was a look of shock.

Lisa pulled out a costume. It wasn't the one she had designed. It was a clown's outfit.

"There's been a mix-up," said Craig.

"It's got to be a mistake," said Gina.
Lisa phoned Spotlight.

The owner spoke. Lisa listened.
Then, Lisa closed her phone.

"Someone changed the order two weeks ago," she said. "Now we have these."

Lisa held up the droopy clown's outfit.

"But the final is two days away," said Tandy.

"I know" said Lisa. She had no idea what to do.

CHAPTER 4
Stitch and Sew

Monica admired her dance outfit.

"I wish I was dancing with you," said Beth.

Monica ignored her. She saw Lisa and Tandy coming.

They looked unhappy. Monica smiled.

"I hear the circus is in town," she said. "Bad luck about your costumes."

Lisa stared at her. She knew Monica was behind this. She just had no proof.

Lisa phoned five costume makers.
The answer was always the same.
"They can't make new outfits in time."

"If only we could make them
ourselves." said Tandy.

"That's it!" cried Lisa. "I'm good at
designing. You, Gina and Franky are
good at sewing. We'll make new
costumes. Craig and Matt can help, too."

Tandy frowned. Had Lisa gone mad?
Lisa phoned the troupe. Everyone came
to her house. Lisa got some paper and
started to draw.

"We need to cut the material. We need
to sew it like this." She held up her
design.

Everyone looked impressed.

"My mum's got a sewing machine," said Franky.

"Mine too," added Gina.

They hurried off to get them. Matt and Craig got scissors, pins and thread. They got beads and sequins.

Tandy showed them how to cut the material. Soon, the sewing machines whirred.

The troupe worked all night. They stitched and sewed.

Finally the sun came up.

Gina tried on her costume. Craig tried on his. They fitted perfectly.

Their costumes looked amazing. They glittered with sequins.

"We've even got noses and wigs," said Craig.

"Now we are the Candy Clowns!"

Everyone was tired. They needed to rest. The final was that night.

CHAPTER 5

Time to Shine

The Glitz final had come.

All but two troupes had danced. Razor Edge was next. Beth watched from the wings.

The drum and bass track started. The troupe began to move. The music was fast and cool. The girls and boys danced together.

The music pounded on and on. Then it stopped. The routine was over.

The crowd loved it.

Monica ran off stage. She punched the air.

"Beat that, clown freak" she said. She pushed past Lisa.

Beth grabbed Monica's arm. Monica shoved her off.

Lisa turned to the Candy Clowns. It was their turn.

"Go out there and dance your socks off," she said.

The music started. Lisa had re-mixed the CD. The troupe walked slowly onto the stage.

They twisted and turned. The music got louder. It got faster. It was like circus-style hip-hop.

The dancers were like acrobats. They whirled and kicked. They tumbled and dived. The music slowed. Then it stopped.

The crowd went wild.

The dancers ran off stage. Lisa stopped to get her breath.

She saw Monica talking to Beth.

Beth looked upset. She was asking Monica something. Suddenly, Monica shouted.

"Stop pestering me. You are such a creep. You're only good to pass on gossip. You're a useless dancer. You'll never be in Razor Edge!"

Beth ran off crying.

Monica didn't see her whispering to a judge.

An announcer walked on stage. "What a great contest," he said. "But Glitz isn't just about dance. It's about fair play. We have been told about dishonesty in the competition. Therefore, Razor Edge is disqualified. The troupe is also banned from competing for one year."

Monica looked as if she had been punched.

The announcer continued. "There is one clear winner tonight," he said. "This troupe took an old theme and made it fresh and original. The winners of the Glitz final are..."

There was a pause. It went on forever.

"Candy Clowns!"
The crowd roared. The Candy Clowns went crazy.

Monica raged with fury. Beth told Lisa everything. She said sorry.

Lisa just smiled. She wasn't worried about Monica.

She had the next competition to prepare for.

Nothing was going to stop the Candy Clowns now.

DANCE

- The history of dance is as old as the history of mankind.

- Dance is an ancient form of expression. It refers to movement of the body. This is usually to rhythmic music.

- In early times, people used dance to mark important occasions.

- They danced to ask for good crops. They danced at births, marriages and funerals. Dance rituals exist in every culture. Many are still used today.

- *Dance is a way of celebrating life.*

- *There are many different forms. Some examples are: ballet, tap, jazz, latin, ballroom, banghra, hip-hop and many more.*

- *Dance is a way of communicating without words. In the 1920s dance was considered as an academic discipline.*

- *Television and film increased people's knowledge of different types of dances. The computer age increased it even further.*

- *Today, the medium of dance is more popular than ever.*

QUESTIONS

- *How many dancers are in Lisa's troupe?*

- *Which troupe does Beth want to join?*

- *What sort of costumes arrive in the box?*

- *What is the name of the costume maker?*

- *What has Lisa done to the music CD?*

- *What is your favourite type of music?*